The Spectre of Hairy Hector

GHOSTLY TALES

Look out for more stories...

The Ghost of Able Mabel

The Spectre of Hairy Hector

Penny Dolan

illustrated by Philip Hopman

■SCHOLASTIC

*To Sonia Benster,
one of life's great encouragers,
with thanks from Penny and Mabel.*

Scholastic Children's Books,
Commonwealth House, 1-19 New Oxford Street,
London, WC1A 1NU, UK
a division of Scholastic Ltd
London ~ New York ~ Toronto ~ Sydney ~ Auckland
Mexico City ~ New Delhi ~ Hong Kong

First published by Scholastic Ltd, 2003

ISBN 0 439 97847 5

Printed and bound by in Denmark Nørhaven Paperback, Viborg

2 4 6 8 10 9 7 5 3

Chapter One

The dawn hung damply in the sky. Two
figures, dressed in black, stood on the steps
of the city church, staring at each other.

The lad wore an ill-fitting jacket. His chin
was set firmly so he didn't show his fear
to anyone, let alone this long-lost aunt who
had appeared at the funeral, and had been
the only one to stand beside him when he
needed it.

Aunt Arcady was certainly not young. Her clothes were plain, and her dark bonnet sat unremarkably on her head, but there was an adventurous glint in her eye that gave him hope.

She peered sharply over her glasses. "So, young Jack," she said, "it seems we are set on some sort of life together."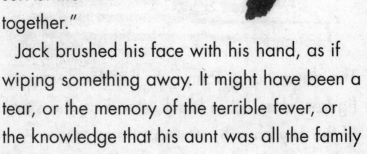

Jack brushed his face with his hand, as if wiping something away. It might have been a tear, or the memory of the terrible fever, or the knowledge that his aunt was all the family he had left in the world.

"Are you ready then?" she continued, more gently.

"Yes, Aunt Arcady, I am," Jack replied, snatching up the small bundle that held all he owned.

"Then we shall soon find out what there is to find out," she said, checking the time on a small silver watch hanging from her waist.

A covered wagon rounded the corner and jolted noisily towards them. The weary farmer at the reins waved a greeting.

"At last!" said Aunt Arcady, raising a gloved hand in reply.

As the horse slowed to a stop, she hoisted up her own bag of belongings, and gave an encouraging smile. "Here we go, Jack," she said, clambering swiftly up on to the wooden seat. "Climb up!"

Jack nipped up, quick as he could, and the wagon set off towards the rain-clouds gathering in the distance.

By late afternoon, the wagon rumbled over the crest of the moorland, and down the long winding road, full of puddles, towards the coast. Suddenly the grey clouds parted, the pale sun shone on far-off waves, and the travellers tasted salt on the wind.

"The sea, the real sea," breathed Jack, his face full of wonder. He only knew the grimy currents of the city river, and how hard it was to row errands between the crowded banks and quays.

"So it is, Jack," Aunt Arcady said, smiling to herself.

Two hours later, the old horse clip-clopped to a halt close by the Anchor Inn. The pair grabbed their bundles, thanked the farmer and stepped down into Seacombe. Aunt Arcady and Jack did not notice the drizzle. They had arrived at last, and now they could hope that the tale they'd been told was true.

It had started with a few printed words, squashed among numerous notices in a large newspaper.

Final Announcement.
Any person, or persons, with the surname Harrible, to contact Silas Splint of Seacombe.

By luck or chance, Aunt Arcady spotted that announcement, and wrote off immediately. Back came a solicitor's letter, and a large scroll, tied with red wax seals and scarlet ribbons.

The scroll told them that, long ago, a great-great-great-uncle, Captain Harrible, had built himself a house in Seacombe. One moonlit night, as Harrible's ship lay moored in the bay, waiting for the wooden dinghy to bring him aboard, a storm sprang up. The wild waves drove the vessel against a reef of rugged rocks. The ship, and Captain Harrible, it seemed, had disappeared.

So Harrible's house stood empty. The letter in Arcady's big bag told them the building had passed from one person to another, and another. Nobody stayed for long. Jack and Aunt Arcady, the last of all the Harribles, were too excited to worry about that.

Arcady glanced over at Jack, and smiled. "Just think! No more cramped attics. No more cold schoolrooms. No more serving and scraping. It's a daydream come true, Jack."

Jack thought about his poor parents, who had grown ill with worry. Then he smiled a little too. "No more one-room-after-another. No more dripping damp. No more rats. Can't hardly believe it, Aunt Arcady," he said. *And no more frightened nights,* he thought.

Because now they *did* have a house – Harrible's House – to be their own home, and that was enough. The misting rain of Seacombe didn't bother them at all.

As they waited on the pavement, Jack saw a man huddled in the porch of the Anchor Inn.

The man's skull was covered in thin, gingery hair, and his pale face blotched with red. A long oilskin coat folded around his gaunt frame, and his bony head stuck out sideways. The man looked rather like an exceptionally ugly umbrella that someone had lost on purpose.

Suddenly the man lurched forward, and gave a small bow.

"Welcome! Silas Splint, of Splint & Sons Solicitors, at your service!" A strange, sneering smile stretched across his yellow teeth. "My family have taken care of everything to do with Harrible's House for years and years and years."

He held a thin hand out towards Aunt Arcady. She merely gave him a crisp smile, and Jack nodded politely.

Just then, a small bundle of cheery folk burst out of the Anchor Inn. As soon as they saw Silas – or was it Jack and Aunt Arcady? – the smiles froze on their faces, and they scuttled off, muttering.

Jack suddenly felt that Splint knew something about Harrible's House that they did not. Something very important indeed.

As Splint took in Aunt Arcady's patched clothing and Jack's ragged jacket, his eyes narrowed. "If that's all you have, we'll be off then." He sniffed, and turned on his heel. "This way!" he snapped, striding briskly off. Jack and his aunt hurried after him, splashing through the puddles in Seacombe's darkening streets. "Who does he think he is?" remarked Aunt Arcady, angrily.

At last, Splint halted by a door. "Here it is!" he declared, and fished a bundle of keys from his pocket. "Harrible's House!"

It was the narrowest house Jack had ever seen, tucked right up against the cliff. It was rather ramshackle, but it still had handsome high windows and ornate iron balconies facing outward to the sea.

Splint turned the key in the lock, and the
door creaked open. The place smelt musty,
as if no one had lived there for a long time.
Odds and ends of filthy furniture were lying
around the old-fashioned room, as if
someone had been searching for something.
Dark wood panelled the walls, but the floor
was nothing better than worn stone slabs.
Splint lit a lantern and set it on the table, but
it gave no warmth.

Aunt Arcady shivered. "Can you light us a fire, Jack?" she asked, looking suddenly weary.

"Course I can," said Jack, but then he saw that the hearth held only a handful of twigs, and the log basket nearby was empty. He spotted a small wooden door in the wall.

"Maybe there's coal in the cellar?" Jack suggested, seizing the basket. Then he saw that the door's enormous keyhole was stuffed tightly with paper and old corks.

"That cellar?" Splint sucked his breath in sharply. "Trust me. Not worth thinking about. Hasn't been opened for years." He rattled the key ring. "There's no key here to fit a lock that size."

"Well then," said Aunt Arcady, pulling her own woollen cloak around her, and settling down in a rickety wooden armchair, "we'll do as best we can until morning. You must be off now, Mr Splint. Thank you for your help – and do leave the keys, won't you?"

Splint's sneering smile faded. "Sleep well, then," he whispered coldly. "I'll be round to see you soon." He left them sitting by the flickering lantern.

Chapter Two

The cry of seagulls woke Jack from his sleep on the wooden settle. The lantern had burnt out, but daylight inched through the cracks in the shutters.

He studied his aunt as she dozed there, with her neatly mended boots, her well-darned skirts and her worn cloak. He was just wondering about what his life would be like with her, when she stretched, opened her eyes and winked at him.

"Could be worse, young Jack," she said, going to the window and flinging the shutters back. "Let's see what there is to see."

Harrible's House looked dirtier by day. There were spiders hanging from the ceiling, and patches of mould on the walls. There was cracked crockery scattered around the kitchen and scullery.

"Won't be so bad once it's cleaned up," Aunt Arcady said, putting on a big blue apron. "I'll see what needs doing."

But Jack, full of curiosity, was already bounding up the steep stairs.

"Hey! Come up here!" he shouted, then hesitated. Had he sounded rude to his new aunt?

But Aunt Arcady's boots were tip-tapping eagerly up behind him. "Well, well!" She beamed. "Our Captain Harrible certainly had some style!"

The first-floor room stretched back amazingly into the cliff. Nobody had closed up the pairs of rickety shutters, so the morning light shone into what was once an elegant drawing room. The sun gilded the rows of dusty mirrors along the walls, and painted the faded carpets with yellow. Even the cobwebs hanging from the carved ceiling seemed like wreaths of gold thread.

Jack was puzzled. This house was much grander than he had expected. Was this why Silas Splint had sneered at them? He imagined Splint pacing about this room, waving his wrist elegantly to and fro like a rich gentleman. *Hmmm!* Jack wondered. Was this something Splint imagined too?

Aunt Arcady opened up the two tall windows. Fresh air blew in and set the cobwebs dancing.

As they stepped carefully on to the balcony, they saw, between the other houses, a patch of bright blue sea.

"This," breathed Aunt Arcady, "is splendid, Jack. Isn't it?"

Up they went again to the next floor, where there was another grand room. All it held was an empty chest of drawers, a cavernous wardrobe, and an exuberant iron bedstead. Much of the mattress had been chewed away by mice, but that didn't seem to bother Aunt Arcady. She beamed, lifted her skirt and apron, and whirled round and round on the faded carpet.

"I'll have this room, if you don't mind, Jack," she cried. "I've spent too many years squashed in stupid sewing rooms, or cooped up in places no bigger than cupboards," she admitted, "or with my elbows red-raw from rubbing along the servants' stairs. This," she breathed, "is almost heaven."

Shredded lace curtains looped the narrow windows, but beyond them, Aunt Arcady's balcony looked out over an even wider stretch of sea.

Grinning, Jack raced further, higher, upwards and found another room. He rushed to the window. From here, he could spy right across the seaside town, and down into the harbour.

The room was in a right state, with sea-birds nesting across the windowsill, and feathers and fishbones scattered down the chimney, but like Aunt Arcady, Jack just didn't care. It was a space, a place just for himself.

Jack tugged at a useful cupboard door, but found instead another flight of stairs. They led to a small attic, which held several old iron-bound chests and trunks, crammed full of bundles of boring cloth. Jack hardly glanced at them. He rushed over to the enormous brass telescope, almost larger than he was, that was set up to look out from this highest window of all.

Jack hauled the smallest trunk over, stood on it, and peered into the lens, but the telescope's wide glass eye was blinded by dust.

He wondered about wiping the lens with his shirt sleeve, but he didn't want to damage the precious glass with dirt-scratches. He shrugged his shoulders, and gave a half-smile. He'd have time to sort out this magnificent machine later.

It was enough, for now, to peer out of the neat window. From here, Jack could watch the whole of the bay, and the surrounding cliffs, and the sailing ships scudding across the glittering waves. It was just brilliant. He stared and stared.

"Hooray for old Harrible!" he chuckled to himself, as Aunt Arcady came puffing into the room.

"I agree," she laughed, staring out to sea. "It's a wonderful sight, Jack, for sure, but it'll be wonderful to have our breakfast too!"

As their footsteps died away down the stairs, the huge brass telescope creaked softly on its mighty mahogany stand.

Chapter Three

Jack and his aunt sat at the old wooden table. Now they'd eaten, all they had left was a small crust of a loaf, a slice of hard cheese and a half-empty packet of tea-leaves. They counted their savings three times, just in case, but the money didn't grow into more. Aunt Arcady put their few coins snugly away in a very small box.

"Well," she sighed, "we can't live on air, young Jack. We'll have to do something, and soon!"

Jack looked downcast. "It's a pity old Harrible didn't think to leave us his fortune as well," he murmured.

"Don't worry," Aunt Arcady said. "Once the house is tidied, we can take in a few lodgers of our own!" She took a bucket out to the yard, to bring in water for the wash-tub.

"Hot water means fires, and fires mean fuel," Jack mused, "and fuel should be kept dry. I must get that cellar door open, surely I must."

For now, Jack brought in a few logs from a pile out in the scullery yard, and set kettles and pans on to boil.

Once the water was hot, they started on the scrubbing and sweeping.

It was a long day, but by nightfall, Harrible's narrow house smelled sweeter and felt cosier.

Although he was exhausted, Jack found a soft clean cloth, and climbed the stairs to the attic again. He stepped up on the small trunk, so he was level with the telescope, and began cleaning the lens extremely carefully.

At last, Jack set his eye to the round brass viewer. He looked through, and saw the constellations shining in the darkness high above, and the waxing moon paint a path of silver across the sea.

"Oh my! Oh my! Bet you wish you could still see this, Captain Harrible," Jack murmured.

At that moment, a very strange thing happened. A great roar echoed though the house, as if someone deep within the building had woken. Jack bolted downstairs as fast as he could, colliding with Aunt Arcady.

"What on earth was that?" she cried.

"It sounded like a..." Jack began, but grew silent.

Together, lanterns in hand, they searched through the gloomy rooms, but found nothing.

"It must have been the wind bellowing
down the chimney," said Aunt Arcady firmly,
as if that was the best thing to believe.

"The wind, surely," agreed Jack quickly,
even though he still had shivers down his
spine. That sound had been almost spooky!

The next morning, as Jack polished the front door, an old woman in a shawl came toiling along the cobbles. She gaped at Jack.

"Well, I'm blowed," she gasped, dropping her basket of vegetables. "Splint's got someone living in the captain's house again."

Jack collected up the rolling carrots and spuds, and popped them back in her basket for her. She gave him a kindly look. "Bet Splint never told you, did he?"

"Told us what?" Jack asked, as they set off up the path.

36

"That Harrible's House is haunted, you daft lummox," she answered. "Each month there comes a terrible, terrifying, tormenting noise! Drives folk mad, so they say!" She leaned closer and her voice dropped to a whisper. "Any Harrible who wants the house has to stay, no matter how bad the haunting gets. If you leave, even for one night, you've lost your chance. Out, with not a farthing or a fishbone to your name!"

"Silas Splint said nothing about that," Jack said, alarmed.

"Nor would he, the sly beggar," the old woman coughed. "Them Splints always were rascals."

"But Aunt Arcady and I are the only Harribles left," Jack explained. "What happens if *we* run?"

"Ho-ho!" The old woman chuckled. "Then Silas Splint claims Harrible's House for hisself. That mean old miser's been a-yearning for that since he was a nipper.

He'll pull the place down, bit by bit, piece by piece, in the hope he finds Harrible's hidden treasure. But he'll do it in the daylight, Silas will, when the noise can't get to him." She grinned at Jack. "So, lad, are you going to skedaddle from Harrible's House?"

"No, we're not! We won't be put out by anything in Harrible's house," Jack insisted loudly, "and as far as treasure goes, what we've found is too old to be sold."

They'd reached the top of the cliff, so Jack handed the basket back to the woman.

"Brave you might sound today, my lad. But soon the moon and the tide will be full," the old woman said, ominously, "and the spectre will be a-raging and a-roaring like the wind in Harrible's House."

Jack gulped, and his eyes widened. A roaring like the wind? A spectre?

"Have you heard any odd noises, then?" the old woman asked, eyeing him curiously. Jack shook his head hard, as if he wanted to shake away last night's scary sounds.

"Well, that's all right then, ain't it?" She grinned, setting off on her way. "But I'll be wishing you both good luck, all the same."

Jack decided not to tell Aunt Arcady about this old wife's horrible tale just yet. If it wasn't true, Aunt Arcady might think him a liar, and then what would become of him? And if it was true, his aunt might up and leave Harrible's House altogether, and then where would he go? He'd just keep a watch on things – and he'd keep a watch on Silas Splint too!

Chapter Four

It was their third evening in Harrible's house. Aunt Arcady was up in the drawing room, cutting some huge old curtains into bed-sheets. As her scissors snip-snapped along, she sang happily to herself.

Jack, in the room below, was trying to keep the fire going. He pushed a long, twisted twig into the grate, and thought about the old woman's words. He felt quite cross at the thought of losing his new home.

"Who's this mouldy old spectre anyway?" Jack asked, loudly. "And what's he bothering us about? That's what I'd like to know."

As if in answer, something clattered down the chimney, and slipped from the fire. It was a huge iron key. It glowed red-hot on the worn stone slabs. Jack watched the key cool and darken, and all at once he knew. It was the key to the cellar!

However and whyever it had come to him, Jack didn't care. Now he could sort out the mystery of the cellar for once and for all.

He might find a
useful stack of coal
down there, for a
start! Jack tugged
the screwed-up
papers and corks
from the keyhole.

He slid the iron
key into the lock.
It fitted perfectly.

The heavy wooden door swung inwards,
revealing a dark space that reached back,
back, back into the cliff, back into absolute
nothingness. Jack seized the lantern in one
hand. He took one step through the door, then
another, and there he was, in the cellar at last!

The lantern shone on up-ended boxes and
upturned trunks, scattered when someone
searched that cellar long before. Whoever it
was had left in a fearful hurry. Now dust
wrapped everything in trailing grey shrouds.
Nobody had been here for a long time.

As Jack edged carefully through the confusion, his breath echoed around him. The air smelt strangely sour, and he heard water dripping somewhere in the dark. The lantern-flame flickered, as if it were about to die on him. "No! Come back to life!" Jack urged.

Slowly, steadily, the flame grew again. As he held the lantern higher, a weird wind came sweeping through the cellar, as if something had been set free from another, awful place. Then Jack sensed that something was moving just beyond the circle of light.

Up out of the darkness loomed a huge figure. It was roaring horridly, and glowing horribly. Long, greasy hanks of matted hair hung from its head, and crusted curls snaked around its shuffling feet. The hideous spectre howled again, raised two hairy arms, and moved towards Jack.

Jack's spine felt like ice, his feet like lead, and he was frozen to the spot. Jack covered his mouth as the foul stench came closer, and closer. Then, all at once, he was yelling and yelling in terror, as loudly as he could. He spun round, and flew from that cellar as fast as he could – but the noise, the thing, was close, close behind him.

Jack leaped out of the cellar, then turned, aghast. The hairy spectre stretched out long filthy hands, and, with a terrifying groan, rose from the cellar, and into the room.

"Aunt Arcady!" Jack yelled at the top of his voice. "Help! Aunt Arcady! Help!"

Aunt Arcady galloped down the stairs, her apron flapping about her, and came to a stop.

By now the ghastly creature was roaming the room, like an animal set free. It bellowed a dreadful chant. **"Beware the Spectre of Hairy Hector! ...Beware the Spectre of Hairy Hector! ...Beware the Spectre of Hairy Hector...!"** it groaned.

Aunt Arcady was already worn-out from cleaning all day. She did not like being interrupted at such a late hour, even by a ghostly spectre.

"Hush your horrid mouth," she shouted. "We heard you well enough the first time." She put her hands on her hips, jutted out her angry chin, and stamped furiously on the stone-slabbed floor. "Now, just tell me one thing. What is it you want?"

The spectre howled as if it was lamenting some terrible tragedy. **"Aaaraaaaaaagh! Aaaraaaaaaagh!"**

One horrible hairy finger was aimed at the wooden panelling just above the fireplace.

Jack paused, thoughtfully, then edged slowly over to where the spectre was pointing. He ran his fingers along the polished wood panels that lined the wall. At first he felt nothing but the usual carving. Then he found it – a tiny notch in the panelling! Jack pressed. With a gentle click, a narrow hideaway sprang open. The spectre groaned even more terribly.

Jack reached rapidly inside, and pulled out a rectangular package, wrapped in rough, hessian cloth.

"Open it up, lad, and let's see it," Aunt Arcady said.

As Jack unfolded the wrappings, the musty hessian fell to threads, revealing an extremely elegant portrait in a gold-edged frame.

The gentleman in the oil painting was a sea captain. He wore a wide-cuffed coat of the very best velvet, decorated with at least twenty shining buttons, and edged with loops of gold braid. Rich lace fell around his proud neck, and he wore a polished pair of buckled red-heeled boots over his breeches. His long lustrous locks twirled elegantly over his shoulders, and a sleek moustache curled wickedly upon his upper lip. A large sword hung from the scarlet sash at his waist, and he brandished a pistol in one gloved hand.

Behind the captain, on the painted sea, sailed a galleon, with cannons blazing, and the skull and crossbones fluttering atop the main mast. Before the captain lay maps and charts marked with red, and a pair of compasses. His right hand wore no glove, just an array of jewelled rings. This hand seemed to point down towards the scrolled charts. The spectre paused, staring longingly at the splendid painting.

Steadily keeping one eye on the apparition, Jack stood up on a handy stool. Carefully he hung the gold-framed portrait back up on a sturdy old hook he'd noticed above the mantelpiece. Then he stepped down.

"Isn't he something to see!" Jack cried, impressed by the handsome image.

Aunt Arcady nodded. "He's certainly a good-looking fellow."

Almost as if it were trying to speak, the creature howled again. Beneath the tangled mess, two red-rimmed eyes glittered, strangely and sadly. Jack stared at the hideous spectre.

Maybe? Could it be? Perhaps? Just possibly?
Was this ghostly, ghastly heap of hair all that
was left of the elegant sailor?

"It's you! It's your portrait," Jack cried.
"You're the spectre of Captain Hector
Harrible!"

An answering roar shook the house.

"No wonder you're unhappy!" remarked
Aunt Arcady briskly. "How can you have let
yourself become such a mess? There's only
one thing to do, sir. Sit on that!"

The creature crouched down on the stool. Aunt Arcady reached into the pocket of her apron, and brought out her sharp scissors. How she did it, Jack never knew, but her silvery blades snipped and snapped and swished through the greasy, ghostly tresses. "Don't you dare move! Spectre or not, your locks need lopping," she snapped. "I'm sure even spooks like to look their best."

As the foul clippings shimmered to the floor, Jack hurried off to find a broom. He wasn't quite sure how you swept up such spectral hair-clippings, but they were too loathsome to be left. It was not as hard as Jack thought, although the tresses did tend to spark and sizzle a bit.

"This is one disgusting head of hair!" Aunt Arcady grimaced, ankle-deep in hairy clippings.

At last the ghostly captain stood shivering in his ghostly, grimy long-shirt. His remaining hair stuck out at odd angles, his moustache looked like rats' tails, and his chin was rough and raggedy.

Jack had already set out a towel, a tub of water and some strong soap for their ghostly guest.

"Captain Harrible, Jack and I are off to our rooms," Aunt Arcady said. She stared sternly and fearlessly through her glasses. The spectre glowered sulkily back. "Less hairy you may be, but you are still horrid. I do not know how you will do it, but wash you must, Captain. Leave everything tidy afterwards. And – ugh! – drop your disgusting body-wear in there."

Aunt Arcady pointed to an empty bucket. The spectre backed away.

"Don't you dare disobey!" Aunt Arcady shook her finger at him fiercely. "GOOD NIGHT and GOOD WASHING to you, sir!" Swiftly she bustled Jack off upstairs.

At the turn of the stairs, Aunt Arcady paused, and grasped desperately at the banister. She was shivering with fright. "Oh, Jack, I was so scared!" she said. "I was so glad you were there!"

"Oh, Aunt Arcady, you were marvellous!" said Jack, and then he told her all about the old woman's warnings.

At last, Jack crawled into bed. He listened to the splashings and sploshings below, and the sound of long-forgotten sea shanties. The moon shone in through his window, growing ever rounder, ever fuller. Aunt Arcady seemed to have set the spectre straight for tonight – but what about tomorrow, when they would have to face the spectre of Hairy Hector again?

Chapter Five

Next morning there was a faintly luminous look to the soap, a weird whiff to the room, and a smelly ring of scum around the bucket where the long-shirt had dropped – and vanished. Jack mopped the worn stone slabs dry again.

"Ah well, not too bad for a ghost, I suppose," said Aunt Arcady, more cheerfully than she felt. Yawning, she pushed the cellar door shut, although she did not lock it.

Around noon, there came a knock on the door. Aunt Arcady went to open it. Silas Splint stood there, hat in hand. He took a step forward but Aunt Arcady stood there firmly. His slippery smile slid away.

"Sleep well?" he enquired. "No noises disturbing you?"

"Nothing but a mouse squeaking in the corner," said Jack, sweetly.

"Nothing but a moth fluttering at the window," smiled Aunt Arcady, vaguely. "It's so pleasant to be in Harrible's House."

"Really?" said Splint, his face darkening. "Well, I'll come calling again very soon."

When Splint had gone, Aunt Arcady stared at the painting of the captain, and gave an anxious sigh.

"What can we do about Harrible, Jack?" she worried. "He's sure to come back tonight. He may not be so hairy, but he's certainly still scary, even if he's scrubbed and shorn." She frowned at the portrait.

"Someone who looked as grand as that won't be content wrapped in my old dressing gown or your patched jacket, Jack." Aunt Arcady shook her head in despair. "Oh dear! Unless Harrible's found some fine clothes, he won't leave us alone."

Jack frowned. Clothes? Cloth? Maybe? He raced up to the attic, and over to the old sea-trunks. He lifted the lids, and started searching through the bundles of cloth.

He found fine old-fashioned shirts and linen and lace collars in one trunk, and embroidered waistcoats and breeches in another. There was everything an elegant gentleman would need. He even discovered a shaving set, and brushes and combs. In the biggest trunk of all, Jack uncovered a magnificent braided coat, and a three-cornered hat. They all needed cleaning or tidying, but Jack carried everything downstairs eagerly.

"Will these do?" he cried.

Aunt Arcady clapped her hands. "Well done, Jack," she cried. "Hand them over. Let's hope the moths haven't munched them to bits!"

As Jack unfolded the wide-cuffed velvet coat for his aunt to inspect, a shower of doubloons rained down on to the stone slabs. Jack and his aunt stared wistfully at the pool of gold coins.

"Pile them on the mantelpiece, Jack," Aunt Arcady said at last. "Captain Harrible can

count his coins back into his own pockets.
I don't think it's good to steal from a ghost."

That night, as the moon grew even rounder, Jack opened the cellar door. An un-hairy spectre sat glimmering malevolently on an upturned barrel, sucking at his soggy moustache. A large towel clung damply around him, and his ghostly feet gleamed in the gloom. His fiery eyes warned of an extremely unpleasant mood. This could be dangerous.

"Well, come out, come out, wherever you are," sang Aunt Arcady lightly, trying to sound as brave as could be. "I've been working my fingers to the bone, Captain Harrible, and I haven't got hours to waste. It's way past my bedtime here."

The spectre shimmered out of the cellar. His eyes scanned swiftly around the room. He saw the clothes Aunt Arcady had laid out across the old chair and table. Some highly respectable underwear. A clean, ironed shirt. A snowy-white neckscarf. A pair of newly stitched breeches. An elegant jacket, with brass buttons gleaming on the newly brushed velvet. Two well-darned socks. A pair of boots that Jack had polished back to brightness.

A gigantic roar echoed through the house again – but this time it was full of delight, as the horrible Harrible gave a most enormous smile.

It was strange to see how, with each item of clothing, the scraggy spectre changed into a ghostly, glimmering gentleman. It was stranger still to see the layers of clothing start to shimmer and shine as he put them on.

Soon Captain Harrible stood there as handsome as his picture – and even more piratical. His long locks curled and twirled, and his smile widened wickedly beneath his smartly sinister moustache. Then he patted his empty pocket, and paused.

"Excuse me," said Jack, quickly, pointing to the glinting gold doubloons, "you'll find your coins there, sir."

Jack tried not to think of how much Aunt Arcady could do with the money. Hector tipped the doubloons noisily, teasingly into his pocket.

Then the spectre eyed his portrait contentedly, almost as if he was gazing at a mirror. He bowed most beautifully towards it, opened his mouth and *spoke*.

"My thanks to you both!" he said, in a voice mysterious and mellow. "But all is not yet done. Today the captain! Tomorrow the ship!"

With a wave of his hat, the ghostly pirate slid slowly back into his cellar.

Chapter Six

Jack spent another restless night, tossing and turning to the sound of swishing swords and terrifying threats. Captain Hector Harrible had found his old sword in the cellar, and was preparing to join his ghostly galleon on the morrow's moonlit tide.

"He'll go, and we'll be left in peace at last," Jack thought, and closed his eyes happily. "All that horrid spectre ever wanted was to get back to his ship."

As Jack drifted off to sleep, he dreamed. He saw Harrible standing ready on the shore, and far out in the bay lay the ghastly galleon at anchor. Jack sensed there was some difficulty he hadn't thought about yet. What could it be? The mysterious worry tolled like a bell in his brain all night.

When daylight came, Jack went off to walk on the cliff to clear his head. At about ten o'clock, Aunt Arcady heard the door latch click, and turned to greet Jack back from his walk.

Instead, she saw Silas Splint standing in the room. He was staring at the magnificent gold-framed portrait of Captain Harrible.

"What's been going on, eh? Where's that from, eh?" Splint stamped his foot hard on the stone floor. "I've been in this house many a time and I've never seen it."

"Maybe Jack and I aren't so *afraid* of what we'll see as you are, Mr Splint. Maybe Jack and I aren't *afraid* of helping," Aunt Arcady smiled, sweetly and smugly, crossing her arms in front of her. "Now, why exactly did you come round?" she asked.

"Came to see if anything was bothering you," Splint said sulkily, chewing his thumbnail.

"Jack and I find our new house just fine. So please leave. Now." Aunt Arcady opened the front door wide. Her skin prickled a warning.

"Well, as everything is so fine," Splint gave a sudden, malevolent sniff, "I'd better give you this."

He handed her a large envelope. Aunt Arcady took it with a puzzled frown.

"It's a bill, Miss Arcady," Splint added. "A bill from Splint & Sons, Solicitors. For looking after Harrible's House for years and years and years," he said, heading for the door. "You can pay me when you're ready – say, by the end of the month?"

Arcady studied the numbers, and gasped. Her face turned as pale as paper. Silas Splint was asking for pounds and pounds, and they had almost nothing. How on earth could she find that money in a month? How on earth could she tell Jack?

As she put the envelope away in her pocket, Arcady bit her lip. She felt more afraid of greedy Splint than of ghostly Harrible.

Chapter Seven

The next night came. Jack, up in the attic, kept watch through the enormous brass telescope. As the sky darkened, the full moon sailed among the billowing clouds. Soon, Jack saw what he half-expected to see.

Over by the rugged rocks that ran along the edge of the bay, something was appearing. Hardly more than a skeleton of broken masts and tattered rigging, the ghost-ship had come to wait for its precious captain. Jack ran downstairs.

It was midnight. Hector's spectre came glimmering through the cellar door one last time. He stood proudly before his piratical portrait, gloating. At last, he raised a ruby-ringed hand, and patted the painting a gentle farewell. Next he bowed most charmingly to Aunt Arcady.

As he moved to the front door, a cunning grin ran across Captain Harrible's ghostly face. "Jack, just walk with me to the shore," he said.

Jack looked across at his aunt, who glanced uncertainly, unhappily back. "If it will help you get back to your ship, Captain Harrible, then I'll come," Jack said, and buttoned his jacket.

"Oh, Jack!" cried Aunt Arcady, her face full of worry. "If you must go, take care, take care!"

She gave him a long, anxious hug. "We've both seen too many sad, lonely times. Harrible's House is nothing to me if I'm on my own." Jack could not find words to answer, so he hugged her too. "I'll keep my wits about me, Aunt Arcady," he promised, and followed the spectre down the winding ways towards the shore.

The moonlight shone brightly on the sea, and the waves rippled gently. Jack's feet crunched down the shingle banks, following in the spectre's silent footsteps.

   Some distance behind, a thin, bony figure
slunk through the night after them. It was
Silas Splint, his eyes maddened with jealousy
and greed, muttering to himself.

"So you sorted out the spectral captain, did you, Jack? Huh! If a lad like you ain't afraid, it can't be much of a spectre after all!" He saw them step across the shingle. "So – you're going to get the reward, eh?" Splint murmured. "Well, if there's any gold going, I'm having some, ghost or no ghost. You'd better watch out, young Jack."

Now the hour of departure was arriving, a strange thing happened. Under the spell of the moonlight, the skeleton ship seemed to change into the beautiful galleon she had once been. Her rotting timbers grew sturdy, and her ragged flags flapped brightly once more. Her huge sails lay against the masts, as if waiting for some ghostly breeze to pass through the bay.

The captain halted where the waves met the shore. He lifted his ghostly hat in the air, and called out to his crew. A strange echoed greeting came back across the water.

"Ah, Jack my lad!" he sighed. "One
moonlit night, I stayed too long at home.
When I heard my ship was gone in the storm,
my heart broke. At last, at last I can join her.
All I need is your help, dear boy!"

Jack suddenly remembered his dream. So
this was what the mysterious worry had been.

The captain smiled enigmatically, and
pointed to a clutch of rowing boats bobbing
by the breakwaters.

"A captain cannot, with honour, row himself to his ship," he said. "You must row for me, Jack." Harrible stepped into the nearest boat, and beckoned.

Jack hesitated. Then, with a heart full of terror, he stepped into the wooden dinghy too. Seizing the two oars, he began to row towards the ghost-ship. Harrible's eyes sparkled mischievously in the darkness.

With each stroke, the small dinghy got closer and closer to the shining ship. The timbers were crusted with carved ornaments, and the fluttering flags were of woven silk. Weird voices rose in chorus – the ghostly crew, singing a welcome for their captain.

Back in the shadow of the breakwaters, another pair of oars slid silently through the water, and another rowing boat moved swiftly across the midnight sea. Another voice softly intoned the ghostly song.

"Ah, gold in *my hand* and such riches galore..." murmured Splint, desperate in his greed.

Chapter Eight

As Jack's rowing boat drew alongside
Harrible's great ship, there was a clunk and
a crash. Down dropped a wooden seat. It
hung there, just above the water, suspended
from four strong ropes. Harrible shrugged his
spectral shoulders, twirled his moustache
absently, and looked rather wistfully at Jack.

"Alas, Jack, 'tis many years since I swung myself aboard by the bosun's chair," he wheedled. "Why don't you try it out for me, boy? It would be tragic if I could not make it aboard after all this time, wouldn't it?"

Jack felt his jaw tighten with fear. Once he was aboard, would he get off again? He'd told Aunt Arcady he'd keep his wits about him, so he opened his eyes as innocently wide as he could.

"I don't quite understand it myself, sir," he said, brightly. "I'd better hold on to the oars."

"Oh, it would be a delight to see a
likely lad like you stand aboard my ship,"
insisted the captain, his hand on his heart.
"Especially when I have chests of good
gold there to reward you with. Wouldn't
you like some gold to take back, Jack?"

Suddenly, a bony figure barged forward,
knocking Jack flat and setting the small
rowing boat swaying violently.

"I'll do it! I'll show you, Captain Harrible."
Splint cried, shoving himself into the wooden
seat. "I'll come aboard and get the gold!"

There was a triumphant cry from above,
and a wooden winch creaked into action.

Swiftly Splint was hauled up on to the deck
of the ghost-ship.

"That's the way to do it! That's the way to get aboard!" chuckled Captain Hector Harrible, tugging mischievously at his moustache. "Ain't it, Jack, my lad?" he whispered, winking triumphantly at Jack. "How could I set sail without one new prisoner aboard my ship?"

Splint's pale face appeared above them, crowing his success and loudly claiming his share of treasure.

Down dropped the wooden chair again. This time, Captain Hector Harrible stood up easily, magnificently, as he could have done all along. Swishing his scabbard aside, he plonked his gorgeous, ghostly self into the seat, lifted his red-heeled leather boots, and swung free.

"On the other hand, if you'd really like to join me, Jack..." he smirked, stretching out a hand.

Jack shoved one oar as hard as he could against the hull of the galleon, pushing with all his might. The rowing boat swirled out of reach.

"HAUL ABOARD! HAUL ABOARD!" Jack yelled out at the top of his voice, listening for the creak of that winch. He did not stop rowing until he saw ghostly hands helping the captain on to his ship.

As soon as the sinister spectre was on deck, it turned. "Well played, Jack! Well played!" Harrible bellowed, his pale face breaking into an amused smile. "Good luck to you, lad, and to your charming aunt."

For a moment Jack drew up the oars, and sat bobbing on the waves, looking back at his strange ancestor.

Captain Hector Harrible stood there, with the full moon shining on his spectral figure, almost as he did in his handsome portrait. Jack gave a rueful grin, and waved back.

"Think of me as I look now, lad, in all my glory! Use your wits, and you'll see where my worldly treasure lies."

The captain raised his hat, and his voice

echoed across the rising surf. "Farewell, Jack! Be happy in my house. Farewell for ever, for ever..."

The huge sails filled out with a weird wind, the massive timbers creaked, and the great galleon surged slowly through the white-crested waves. Jack saw a bony figure stretch out desperate arms, shrieking in horror above the rattling of chains.

As the ship slid across the silvery disc of the moon, it again took on its ghastly shape. Jack heard the strange singing long, long after the ghostly skeleton of the ship had melted into the rising mist.

As Jack rowed the last lonely lengths to the shore, he thought of all that had happened. Did the captain know that was what Splint would do all along? Jack would never know. All he had left from the adventure was the captain's portrait, hanging high on its hook.

Jack called the image to mind. He sighed, he thought – and then he laughed. They'd been wrong. Hector Harrible was not pointing at the charts and maps in the painting, not at all. Harrible's beringed hand was pointing out of the frame, down at the worn stone slabs on the floor of his house. That was where Harrible's hoard of treasure lay! That was what the spectre had been telling him! Jack hugged the idea happily to himself as he rowed.

As the small boat glided towards the

shallows, Jack turned and saw a single figure in a long cloak, high on the shingle, waiting for him. It was Aunt Arcady, holding a lantern high, guiding him safely to shore, and safely home.

GHOSTLY TALES

Prepare to shiver – the ghosts are here!
The strangest, scariest, *spookiest* spirits – back
from the past to haunt your bookshelf!

Look out for the next book in this shivery series!

The Ghost of Able Mabel

Able Mabel is huge and horrible.
She's a thief and a pirate ... and she's a ghost!
Many years ago she stole a box of gold
from Sam's old grandad – and now Sam
wants it back. No matter that Mabel won't
let it go without a fight...

Young Hippo
**Terrific stories, brilliant characters
and fantastic pictures – try one today!**

There are loads of fun books to choose from:

Jan Dean
The Horror of the Black Light

Alan MacDonald
The Great Brain Robbery

Penny Dolan
The Ghost of Able Mabel
The Spectre of Hairy Hector

Mary Hooper
Mischief and Mayhem!
Spooks and Scares!

Frank Rodgers
Head for Trouble!
Haunted Treasure!